HALLOWEEN NIGHT

BY MARJORIE DENNIS MURRAY

ILLUSTRATIONS BY BRANDON DORMAN

Greenwillow Books
An Imprint of HarperCollins*Publishers*

Halloween Night
Text copyright © 2008 by Marjorie Dennis Murray
Illustrations copyright © 2008 by Brandon Dorman
First published in 2008 in hardcover; first paper-over-board edition, 2010.
All rights reserved. Manufactured in China.
For information address HarperCollins Children's Books,
a division of HarperCollins Publishers, 10 East 53rd Street, New York, NY 10022.
www.harpercollinschildrens.com

Digital art was used to prepare the full-color art.
The text type is 18-point Esprit Book.

Library of Congress Cataloging-in-Publication Data
Murray, Marjorie Dennis.
Halloween night / by Marjorie Dennis Murray ; illustrations by Brandon Dorman.
p. cm.
"Greenwillow Books."
Summary: Loosely based on "The Night Before Christmas," this rhyming story
tells of a group of animals, monsters, and witches who prepare such a frightening
Halloween party that their expected trick-or-treaters all run away.
ISBN 978-0-06-135186-0 (trade bdg.) — ISBN 978-0-06-135187-7 (lib. bdg.) —
ISBN 978-0-06-201293-7 (pob bdg.)
[1. Haunted houses—Fiction. 2. Halloween—Fiction. 3. Parties—Fiction.
4. Stories in rhyme.] I. Dorman, Brandon, ill. II. Title.
PZ8.3.M937On 2008   [E]—dc22   2007027686

10 11 12 13 14 SCP 10 9 8 7 6 5 4 3 2

 Greenwillow Books

To my sister Leilani, with love and best witches
—*M. D. M.*

Dedicated to my son Sam, who is often
found scribbling away by my side
—*B. D.*

'Twas Halloween night, and all through the house
Every creature was stirring, including the mouse;

The walls were aflutter with little brown bats,
While hordes of black spiders crept out of the cracks.

By the fire in the kitchen, the witch stirred her brew;
To make it more smelly, she threw in a shoe.

Stiff-legged zombies awoke from the dead,
As moth-eaten mummies arose from their beds.

The pumpkins all grinned
with ghoulish delight,

As little green creepies
made treats for the night.

Into each party bag
they dropped four crunchy legs,

A handful of grubs,
and eight rotten eggs.

The ghost in the parlor played softly off-key,
As a bevy of banshees served moldy green tea.

Ogre and Olaf set up the buffet
With freshly picked bugs
And the soup of the day.

When up on the gable the ravens appeared,
Ready to cry when the tricksters drew near.

Then just as the moon shed light on the path,
The witch and her ravens heard somebody laugh,
And like tiny moths drawn into the flame,
The tricksters appeared at the end of the lane—

A witch, a toad, a ghost, and a bat,

A vampire, a mummy, a yellow-eyed cat,

A fairy, a ghoul, and a plump little rat.

"Quick!" cried the witch.
"They're coming this way!
Take the pot off the fire!
Unveil the buffet!"

Then laughing and giggling the children all came,
Their feet treading lightly over the lane,
All silly and giddy and looking for sweets,
All shouting together,

TRICK OR TREAT!!!

"Come in!" said the witch. "Please be our guests.
Come to our party! We've put out our best!"
Into her parlor the children all peeked,
So eager to see the Halloween treats.
But what they saw on that shadowy night,
Made each little trickster shiver with fright!

Mummies and harpies and creepy green things,
Fish tails, and stinkbugs, and dragonfly wings;
Newts and toads and lizards and mice,
Flies in the soup and crickets on ice;
A ghost in the parlor and bats in the den,
The witch's pet monster *outside* of its pen;
And Ogre and Olaf and all of their friends!

From the ten little tricksters came ten little shrieks,
And away they all ran down the cobblestone street,
Dropping their bags and spilling their treats.

EEK! AHHH! YOW! YIKES! YELP! YEEP! GAA! HEEP! HELP! WHOA!

So Ogre and Olaf and all of the rest,
Enjoyed Halloween night without any guests.

They each took home some leftover legs,
Some grubs and bugs and lizards and eggs,
And all agreed on that night, as they left,
That . . .

this was the very best
Halloween yet!